anythink

D0570853

cloverleaf books™

Off to School

William's 100th Day of School

by **Lisa Bullard**

Illustrated by **Mike Byrne**

M MILLBROOK PRESS • MINNEAPOLIS

For Kris: fantastic teacher,
fantastic sister-in-law—L.B.

For Harry: the first of many—M.B.

Millbrook Press
A division of Lerner Publishing Group, Inc.
241 First Avenue North
Minneapolis, MN 55401 USA

For reading levels and more information, look up this title at
www.lernerbooks.com.

Main body text set in Slappy Inline 22/28.
Typeface provided by T26.

Library of Congress Cataloging-in-Publication Data

Names: Bullard, Lisa, author.
Title: William's 100th day of school / Lisa Bullard.
Other titles: William's hundredth day of school | William's one
    hundredth day of school
Description: Minneapolis : Millbrook Press, [2018] | Series:
    Cloverleaf books—off to school | Includes bibliographical
    references and index.
Identifiers: LCCN 2016051897 (print) | LCCN 2017000060
    (ebook) | ISBN 9781512439359 (lb : alk. paper) | ISBN
    9781512455823 (pb : alk. paper) | ISBN 9781512451047 (eb
    pdf)
Subjects: LCSH: Hundredth Day of School—Juvenile literature.
Classification: LCC LB3533 .B85 2018 (print) | LCC LB3533
    (ebook) | DDC 372.18—dc23

LC record available at https://lccn.loc.gov/2016051897

Manufactured in the United States of America
1-42148-25421-12/1/2016

TABLE OF CONTENTS

Chapter One

99 Days and Counting

I can't wait for tomorrow! We're having a big parade for the 100th day of school, and I'm bringing something special for show-and-tell.

Actually, I'm bringing 100 somethings!

The 100th day is a celebration just for schools. Since the celebration is about school days, holidays and weekends aren't counted.

5

On the first day of school, my teacher,
Mr. Zimmer, wrote "1" on the calendar.

FEBRUARY

SUN	MON	TUE	WED	THUR	FRI	SAT
	1	2	3	4	5	6
7	8	9	10	11	12	13
14	15	16	17	18	19 **99**	20
21	22	23	24	25	26	27
28						

Friday was day 99.

Tomorrow is day 100. We'll be 100 days smarter than we were on the first day of school!

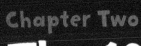

Chapter Two

The 100th Day of School

The 100th day of school is finally here, and it's time for show-and-tell! Emma has 100 **googly eyes.**

No one is surprised by George's box of 100 purple things.

Purple is his favorite color!

We compare our items. My 100 marbles are a lot heavier than Abbie's 100 cotton balls.

We practice skip counting by 2s. "2, 4, 6."

Skip counting is a way to count more than one number at a time.

Then we skip count by 10s. "10, 20, 30."
Counting by 10s is a shortcut to get to 100!

Chapter Three

100 All Through the Day

In the gym, we do 10 exercises, 10 times each, which equals 100 times!

Then we practice marching for the 100th day parade.

Back in class, our small groups write 100 words we've learned this year on big parade banners.

- GIVE YOUR FRIEND A HIGH FIVE.

- HOLD THE DOOR OPEN FOR SOMEONE.

- SAY SOMETHING NICE TO A FRIEND.

Then we all work together to think of 100 ways to be kind.

My crown is for the
parade too. I used 99
sunflower seeds to
spell my name, William.

I started with 100 seeds, but then I thought of one more way to be **kind!**

Day 101?

100th DAY

RIEND A HIG

R OPEN FOR

RIEND

DAY 100

The parade ends our big day!

BRIINNGG! The bell tells us the 100th day is finished. At first, I'm sad.

Students still have many more days of school after the 100th day.

But then I think: tomorrow we can celebrate day 101!

21

Happy 100th Birthday!

What would life be like on your 100th birthday? It's hard to know for sure, but it's fun to imagine!

What You Will Need
paper
coloring tools, such as colored
    pencils, crayons, markers, or paint

What You Will Do
Make a picture of how you imagine things will look at your 100th birthday celebration. Here are some questions to get you started:

- What will you look like when you turn 100?

- What kinds of clothes will people wear?

- What kinds of machines will people use?

- What kinds of homes will families live in?

- What special things will people do to celebrate birthdays?

calendar: a chart that shows the days, weeks, and months

celebration: a special way of marking an important event. A celebration may involve special activities or foods.

compare: to look at two or more items to see how they are alike or different

equals: the same as

100th day of school: a special celebration that takes place when students reach the 100th day of school for the year

skip counting: a way to count more than one at a time, such as counting by twos or counting by 10s

BOOKS

Bullard, Lisa. *Sofia's First Day of School.* Minneapolis: Lerner Publications, 2018. The countdown to day 100 starts on day one! Here's a story about the first day of school.

Hills, Tad. *Rocket's 100th Day of School.* New York: Random House, 2014. Rocket had collected 100 things for the 100th day of school, but something has gone wrong. Check out this story to find out how Rocket fixes his problem.

Miller, Reagan. *100th Day of School.* New York: Crabtree, 2010. Discover lots of different ways to celebrate the 100th day of school.

WEBSITES

Adventure Man and the Counting Quest
http://www.abcya.com/adventure_man_counting.htm
Practice skip counting with Adventure Man!

100th Day of School
http://www.starfall.com/n/holiday/hundredthday/play.htm?f
Work on counting to 100, along with other fun activities, on this website.

Peg's Pizza Place
http://pbskids.org/peg/games/pizza-place
Practice counting by helping to make pizza at Peg's Pizza Place.

LERNER SOURCE
Expand learning beyond the printed book. Download free, complementary educational resources for this book from our website, www.lernerresource.com.